W9-CUL-625

Wasn't Tomorrow Wonderful
Copyright 2013
By John Stilwell

Other books

Nonfiction Books:

100 Ways to Save a Dollar without Lowering Your Lifestyle
The Independent Author's Handbook - Second Edition
The Stilwell Family Cookbook (Free)

Science fiction:

Adrift on a Sea of Stars
Beyond the Galactic Core
Earth not Forgotten
The Galactic Time Trap (2016)
The Puppy of Doom and Other Stories
In the Image of Gods
Tank (audiobook) in MP3 and CD

Blogs:

JohnStilwell.blogspot.com
StilwellFamilyCookbook.blogspot.com
Techwatch2.blogspot.com
SmartTaveller2.blogspot.com

What if, suddenly, everybody in the world had access to a limited form of time travel?

What if they could send an email to themselves exactly one month into the future, or one month into the past?

How would it change society?

It would *certainly* cause trouble.

This is a collection of three short stories: The first is about the average person's experience once handed the ability to talk across time. If you have read the book, "The Puppy of Doom", you will recognize the character Albert. The second st about a petty crook. In he third story, the ɼ has to come to grips with an unwelcome

To Csaba. Thank you for the long hours discussing story ideas.

Table of Contents:

You've got time-mail!

FROM: Me ⏷ , TO: Me ⏷

DATE: One month in the future ⏷

Don't date her. She's crazy!

Reply to the ○ Future or the ○ Past

Message:

[Reset] [Submit]

1 Message, 0 unread, 1 t-mail is available to send

Wasn't Tomorrow Wonderful!

© Temporal Industries

Albert's Time Mail

Albert was on his hands and knees in his tiny back yard, working on his rock garden. Climate change meant that summer was drought and winter had become the growing season. Water needed to be conserved; so he had laid a grid of flat rocks sheltering the moisture in the ground between the plants, which was a technique that went back several centuries; at least to when Easter Island's ecology had started to collapse. Recently, rocks had become more popular than the traditional mulch.

Inside a small yard, a knee-high chicken-wire fence surrounded a modest garden. Inside was Albert and outside was his bio-pet named Buddy. Buddy wandered back and forth, looking for mischief to get into. Given a chance, Buddy would eat all of the plants. He even liked cotton socks. Albert had learned the hard way that it was important to keep his unattended natural fabric based clothes out of Buddy's reach.

Albert loved his neon-green, chicken-sized Tyrannosaurus Rex. Buddy loved him back. Designed by committee as the "it" Christmas gift, Buddy was as playful as any puppy and nowhere as needy. The same long list of genetic modifications that gave the little animal big, forward-looking doe-eyes and a comical look also had made its line vegetarians with flat teeth. The dinosaur-inspired bio-pets had been all the rage a couple of years back. Then the toy company had surprised the world with talking dogs and opened a nasty, legal 'can of worms' they hadn't expected. Were talking dogs entitled to civil rights? Was the toy company trying to breed a slave race? The angry litigation was still building steam. Only time would tell if the toy company would survive.

Albert's sunglasses rang. He touched one side of them, "Hello?"

"It's me," a familiar voice greeted. It was his mother. There was no video displayed in his eyeglasses, only sound next to his ears. Mom didn't like video phone calls.

"Hi, me," Albert joked back.

"Ha. Ha. You need a new joke son. You need to swap it out for a new one every decade or so."

"I will, mom. So what's up?"

"You didn't call me! You *always* call me, when the next big shiny toy catches your eye."

Albert stood up cautiously and straightened his back with a groan. "I don't follow." It was true that he had to have every crazy new gadget before everybody else. Usually they turned out great. The robot had been big trouble, but he loved Buddy and was happy with the gene therapy that had given him hair on his head and six-pack abs. His latest purchase was his glow-in-the-dark bike. It went well with the glow-in-the-dark ceilings he had added to the hallways and bathrooms. Had he forgotten to tell her? No, he was sure he had. *Had he?*

"The bike?" he ventured.

"No silly, the time mail."

Time mail? "What's time mail?"

There was silence over the phone. "You mean I know about something before you?" Laughter poured forth from the two temples of Albert's smart eyeglass phone. "This is a first. You are always calling me with what's new. My turn. Time mail! Time travel email! It's all over the news."

Albert collapsed outside the garden, onto the patio and into a cross-legged sitting position. *What was she talking about?* He needed a second to absorb the words. Time travel email? Impossible! Was this a joke? It wasn't April. Wait. He tapped the side of his sunglasses. The date appeared in the lens in front of his eyes. Nope. It wasn't April Fool's Day. "The news?"

"Yes, honey."

Albert gestured with his hands and spoke a couple of key words. The eyeglasses responded and he surfed the Internet. Every news outlet had a story. It was the top story on Reuters. It read that a new email service had been unveiled: claiming to allow you to send emails back and forth to yourself, exactly one month into the future. The secret commercial venture had taken ten years. The technology was based on quantum entangled rubidium atoms and the mothballed particle accelerator outside of Chicago. The accelerator was used to time-dilate half of the enabled atomic pairs by thirty days. "Wow," was all Albert could say.

The whole following week was hell. He couldn't keep his mind on work. All he could do was think about the Time Mail. He couldn't wait to use it himself. Unlike the free email services he'd grown up with, this cost real money to use. It was a flat fee, and a charge per email sent. Whenever he tried to login to open an account and pay the hefty fee, web pages would time out before he could get through the process. There were stories on the TV and the radio about everybody rushing to use the service. Several were about the company's servers constantly crashing due to the heavy load. All he knew was that the login started with a video of HG Wells climbing into his time machine and rushing into the future. The site would then hang, sometime during the video or halfway through the sign up forms. It was maddening!

Then it finally happened. It was in the wee hours. The application finally went through and he had his account! He was redirected to a different web address and he read the instructions. It wasn't complex. Any email he sent "Forward" would appear in his mailbox in exactly thirty days in the future. Any email he sent "Backwards" would appear in his mailbox exactly thirty days in the past. He could **not** send to anybody but himself. He could only send one email a day and it could **not** be more than twenty characters. The letters had to all be upper case. The web instructions explained there was a limited amount of data that could be transmitted per day. Once the service's quota was used up, for the day, time mails would be buffered, to be transmitted the following day. There was an apology and a statement from the company that "increased data volume" was planned.

He finally found himself on the web page that displayed his mailbox. Time Mail's motto, "Wasn't Tomorrow Wonderful!" was displayed in the corner of the window in ornate letters. His mailbox was empty. His "Send mail backwards" button was grayed-out, with a timer next to it. "You can send it in 30 days," the web page promised.

He clicked on "Send email forward". An email edit window opened. Twenty letters available. What to say. "Hi from the past?" Each letter cost money. That gave you incentive not to chatter needlessly. But he had to try. He had to experience the thrill of talking across time. What to say to the future him? He could scribble a note, and put it in an envelope and post it on the cork board in the kitchen for thirty days *for free*. What to do?

Wait! The inbox icon. It had a picture of an envelope in it. Did that mean he had a letter to read? He clicked on the icon. The in-basket opened up. There were the images of two letters in it. Albert feverishly opened the first one. It wasn't from the future. It was a welcome letter. He clicked on the second and it opened. The title stated, "From the Future!" with a date and time stamp. The body of the message read, "COMDY BAD SEE ACTION". At the bottom, it had the company logo. "Wasn't Tomorrow Wonderful."

Did it mean that the comedy club was bad and he should instead see an action film? What action film? He really wanted to go to see the stand-up comic on Thursday. He had received a message from himself, from the future. It was the most amazing feat of humanity and it was a critique about a stage act. Imagine that. He pondered on this for a while, then got undressed and fell into bed. "Goodnight, Buddy."

Thursday arrived and he went to the comedy club anyway. The MC told the same jokes as last time. Boring. Then a sprinkler head in the ceiling broke and everybody got soaked. Chaos! It was a miserable evening. He should have skipped the show. The next day, at work, one of the people he was talking to suddenly mentioned an action movie they liked. It sounded mildly interesting. He forgot about it, five minutes later.

Over the next two weeks, he received a message almost daily. None were very exciting. They were mainly about bad TV shows to avoid and impending door dings in his car. As excited he was to read the t-mail, it was all petty stuff. *Is that what peoples' lives mainly are?* He secretly wanted t-mail knowledge from the future to make him a super hero! *Was his life just a sequence of petty moments?* It was depressing to think about.

Still, the concept was exciting. It was a solution to Robert Frost's poem, "The Road not Taken". We all experience having to make choices in life, never knowing what it would have been like if we'd taken the other path instead. T-mail let you walk down one path for a month, then turn back and try another path it you wanted. It let everybody try out the different options, and letting you keep the best. It let everybody 'undo' some of their mistakes. It must be making a lot of lives better.

The news was all a-buzz with t-mail stories. One was about a class action lawsuit against Temporal Industries. The Plaintiff was the Association of Independent Palm Readers and Rootworkers. *What's a rootworker?* They were complaining that time mail was wrecking their livelihood. Albert was much more amazed to learn that there was an organization of palm readers than he was about the lawsuit.

There was an intellectual debate about t-mail's various paradoxes. If you warn yourself about making a mistake, so you never make it, *how can you know to warn yourself?* There didn't seem to be an answer to this. Other than - it was happening. It was possible.

If you have three options, could you change your mind twice? How could you test it?

One theory was that each decision shifted *that* person into an alternate reality. The warning from the future **not** to make the past decision continues to exist, because **it** came from your 'future self' in the previous reality.

Yet another line of argument was that the previous physicist was an idiot, and that the grandeur and vastness of the multi-verse couldn't care less, if an insignificant speck of dust, called a human, buttered their morning toast or not.

At this same time, Albert was going through a dating dry spell. He met plenty of women and was reasonable at the art of flirting. He would get the occasional phone number; but when he'd call the next day to arrange the date the woman was no longer interested.

He met Brenda at a bar. It was a Thursday night. He asked her to dance. They laughed. Brenda was a tall buxom woman with long brunette hair. When they slow-danced for the first time, he meant to put his arms around her waist but missed. She was taller than he was used to, and instead of her waist, his hands rested on her bottom. Surprised, Albert immediately let go. "I'm sorry," he gasped. "I didn't mean to! It was an accident!"

She didn't look surprised. The music was loud and throbbing. Her face was close to his. "Shhh," she said quietly. "It's OK. Just hold me tight. Maybe I'll let you do that again later." She clung to him on the dance floor for what felt like forever. They melted together. The night flew away. She wrote her number on the palm of his hand and breathed into his ear, "I really hope you call me."

The next day, he called her after work. Brenda giggled and they laughed. She was so easy to talk to. "I'd love to have dinner with you. I'm available Saturday night," Brenda told him. They only hung up after each of them said, "Bye," several times. Neither wanted to hang up the phone first. Albert walked on clouds all day on Friday. Saturday at noon, she sent a text message to him, saying that she had to cancel the date. She had lost interest in Albert. He didn't know what he had done wrong.

The next week, he met Laura in the vegetable section of the grocery store. It was a Wednesday. She was a pretty blonde with short hair, and a pale northern European complexion. She wasn't very curvaceous, but was beautiful in an athletic way. Albert pretended to be clueless about where the mushrooms were. She walked him over to them and pointed out the selection. He made a joke. She laughed. There was a sparkle in her eye.

"Can I shop with you?"

Laur[...] [...]ged with a coy smile. "Sure."
They walked [...] lked up and down every aisle.
"I hav[...] [...]thing on my list."
She n[...] [...]s at Albert. "Me too."
"I'm i[...] h to go home. Want a cup of coffee?" He [...] his thumb at the little coffee shop in the co[...] he grocery store. Laura nodded yes. He bough[...] appuccino. He had an espresso. They [...] chocolate-dipped biscotti and the story of the[...] In the end, she sat very close and spoke her p[...] mber into Albert's smart eyeglasses. The [...] le phone recorded it. Then she left.

Albert ca[...] next evening to ask her out on a date. She di[...] wer, so he left a message. Two days later, h[...] ed a text message explaining that she didn't wa[...] out with him.

Work was [...]. Albert had a new boss who was piling ex[...] on him and not giving him any extra time to g[...] e. He was unhappy at the office. At home, he [...] 't get a date. Albert was in a funk. There was [...] ew on the Internet and he wasn't able to get on [...] ne mail. He needed his 'daily fortune cookie[...] from the future more than ever! Net conge[...] as causing dropped Internet connections. [...] e time mail servers went down for four da[...] news said it was because there were too [...] sers.

It was five days [...] efore all of the problems went away. [...] mail had acquired significant additional re[...] from the Cloud. Temporal Industry's CE[...] gized in a web cast for the outage, and promised that, going forth, they could handle the load.

Albert had no t-mail the first day but did the second. "CNCL OSUN BAD TRAFIC". It took Albert awhile to figure it out. He finally concluded that it said, "Cancel Ocean, bad traffic". In the early days of text messaging on cell phones, it was hard to type the letters. Abbreviations, acronyms and bad spellings eased the pain. With time mail, this same solution was reborn. New ideas and old text messaging dictionaries were being emailed back and forth. Acronyms like LOL for 'laugh out loud' failed to make a comeback. It didn't fit the nature of time mail. T-mail had found a home as the new daily horoscope. It was tailor written by you, just for you.

Saturday morning came and Albert didn't head to the ocean. He slept in, instead. When he woke up, he cooked bacon, hash browns and fried egg breakfast. He took it to the living room and flopped on the sofa. His breakfast was on a TV tray. Next to him on the sofa was a bowl filled with a vegetable salad. It had carrots, celery and lettuce. It was Buddy's breakfast. The bowl also had some cherry tomatoes. Buddy loved tomatoes.

Buddy's short arms were a caricature of a tyrannosaurus with stubby fingers. They weren't useful for much. He couldn't climb the sofa on his own. Albert lifted the little animal up to sit next to him. Buddy accepted the help gleefully.

"TV on! Local news," Albert spoke to the room. The TV obeyed. There had been a terrible accident on the highway and the backup was twenty miles long. The Bay Bridge was closed. Frustrated commuters, giving up and driving down the shoulder or racing too fast - once they escaped the massive backup - were getting into other accidents. It was a mess! Albert petted Buddy's head and the animal crunched on a carrot. He loved time mail.

The news changed to a report about the Astrologers' Guild joining the Palm Readers' class action lawsuit against time mail. He then surfed to the movie website and hunted for a good action movie. *What was the one he'd been told about a few weeks back?* It was at the tip of his tongue.

Albert's new boss continued to be difficult. Albert's stress level was high. After work, he went to Happy Hour and sat at the bar. He talked to a couple of people. Small talk. Brief chitchat.

A woman sat on the recently vacated stool next to him. "Eh," she articulated as she nodded to him.

Albert nodded back. He was lost in his own problems.

"What you drinking?" she asked.

Albert looked at her for the first time. She was kind of sexy, in an action comic book superhero kind of way. Her hair was short, white and spiky. It screamed of adventure. Her earrings were long and thin triangles, almost like spears. Her eyes were striking. She had cat eyes. Gene therapy to body modify was common enough. Albert had done it to get a muscle builder's body and a full head of hair. Within limitations, anybody could be handsome and beautiful if they wanted. Some, like this woman wanted to stick out in a non-traditional way.

"What are you drinking?"

"Black and tan." Albert lifted his glass in a half salute.

Her eyes were so distracting. Every time she blinked, his attention was drawn to her cat eyes.

She leaned close and her shoulder brushed Albert. "Bartender! Hey! I'll have what he's having!"

They had a few drinks. She ordered shots for the two of them to celebrate each others hell days being over. The rest was a blur. Albert remembered them doing a shot where one then kissed the other to share the drink. It ended in a kiss. Then there was just plain kissing. He recalled rushing after her, into her car. Her autopilot had driven the two of them to her apartment. There was hot, sweaty rolling back and forth on the floor together. *Where had his clothes gone? Where had the night gone?* "Oh God. I have to go to work in four hours. How am I going to get home?"

Her face was buried in the pillow on the bed. "Stay," she muttered sleepily.

"But we have to get up soon. I have to get back to my car." Albert rolled out of bed and sought out his clothes. They were scattered everywhere, like there had been an explosion. "Where am I? Can you drive me to my car?" *What was her name?*

The woman groaned. "Stay. Sleep."

"I need to go," Albert pleaded. "What time do you start work?"

"I don't."

"Don't what?"

"I got fired a week ago."

"Why?"

"I slept with my boss's wife," she mumbled.

Albert took a moment to process that. He then started to dress. "I still need to go. Can you take me to my car?"

"Take a taxi."

"Really?"

"Yes"

"Truly?"

"Come to bed or get out," she mumbled and rolled over in the bed and burrowed deeper under the blankets.

Albert ordered a taxi with his smart eyeglasses phone. He sat on the stoop outside the apartment building in the dark, until it arrived.

That was how Albert started another crappy day. That night he had a time mail that warned, "CAT WOMAN RUN AWAY".

He had no date that weekend. It was just Buddy and him in his PJs, on the sofa watching movies again. He put his smart phone eyeglasses in another room. The cat woman had been calling him every five minutes for hours.

It was about one in the afternoon when he had a thought. It was a worrisome thought. It was bred from his t-mail that warned him about the crazy cat woman. *Could that be it? No. Couldn't be.* He retrieved his eyeglasses and put them on. The display embedded in the lenses presented a list of phone numbers. He scrolled through his calling history. Success. "Call Brenda," he commanded.

"Hello?"

"Hi Brenda. This is Albert."

There was a pause. "From the bar? I'm sorry. I'm just not interested."

"That's OK. I just have one question."

She sighed. "OK. Shoot."

"You really liked me in the bar. Why did you cancel the date?"

Brenda weighed her options for a moment. She decided to go with honesty. "I told myself to."

"What? Told yourself? Time mail?"

Brenda paused. "Yes."

"Why?"

Another pause. "I would have slept with you that same night. I'd then feel like a tramp the next day."

"But you didn't have to on the first date."

"Yeah. Then I got another future gram. I'm supposed to meet Steve next. It might be tonight. I'm not sure. But it's very soon. Sorry. I'm supposed to be more interested in Steve."

"Oh," Albert muttered. He had been dumped before actually having a girlfriend. That was a new land speed record.

"If it means anything, I had a time mail telling me I was going to meet you! That's why I was so forward when we first met."

Knowing his suspicion was true didn't help any. He then called Laura. She also had received a time mail from her future self, saying that she was going to meet Albert. She later received an email that after four dates Albert hadn't proposed, so she refused the first date. She really wanted to get married! She didn't want to waste her time on men that weren't serious.

Albert was depressed all weekend. With the efficiency of time mail, nobody could get a date anymore! But the cat woman? No wait. She'd jumped him before he had a chance to warn himself. She'd dragged him into bed hoping to get him to stay. She hoped he'd ignore her craziness. He hated time mail. He hated it even more when it occurred to him that she wasn't getting dates either. Instead of taking the lesson to behave more normal, she was becoming more extreme. T-mail was making some lives worse.

Albert was completely miserable at work. His boss was dumping too many tasks on him. One day he was given three "Drop everything and get this done by noon!" reports at the same time. He wanted to quit. He would have too; but the night before he had received a t-mail saying, "DO NOT QUIT". He felt trapped. *Beyond his stress and frustration, was his life also boring without uncertainty?* He wasn't sure.

The economy was erratic. The news was full of time mail stories. Society was stumbling towards a new normal. There were fewer accidents as more people were learning to religiously check their daily self-written temporal horoscopes. Insurance companies profits were skyrocketing as the number of claims plummeted. Other businesses were going under. People wasted less money, which meant they were spending less. Some industries, like casinos, were getting hammered as their customers were suddenly winning too often. *Could there be a recession about to happen?*

There were net congestion troubles again. Access to time mail was spotty. One hacker activist group was trying to shut down time mail, while another hacker activist group was cyber attacking the first, to keep time mail up. Whatever the new normal would be, it hadn't been reached yet.

It was in the wee hours. Saturday had barely started when Albert stumbled into the house. He had gone straight from work to Friday Happy Hour, then with friends to the next bar, until the bartender turned on the bright lights and shouted, "Go home!" Albert awkwardly walked up the half flight of stairs, turned down the hall and into his bedroom.

Buddy was asleep in the corner in his little doggie bed. "Have to check the mail," he said to himself aloud. In his inebriated fog, listening to his own voice gave him a gauge of how drunk he was.

He clumsily logged into his time mail account and squinted at the screen. There was the inbox icon. It had a picture of an envelope in it. He had t-mail! He clicked on the icon. The inbox opened up. He clicked on the envelope and it opened. The title said, "From the Future!" The body of the message read, "BUDDY CHOKES ON TIE". At the bottom, was the company logo, "Wasn't Tomorrow Wonderful!"

Albert logged out. He was completely exhausted. He was still in his work clothes. Frantic, he had to check on Buddy. He awkwardly stood up. Buddy was asleep in his bed, on the floor in the corner of his room. Relief. He was so tired. *When would Buddy choke on a tie?* There was no date. *Maybe tomorrow he would get that in the next message*, he worried.

A strange noise woke him up. He opened his eyes and looked groggily around. It wasn't time to get up yet. He had another half-hour, so he nestled back into his big pillow. He then heard rustling. It stopped. Must be Buddy moving around. He often woke up before the alarm. But something felt wrong. He was in bed. He didn't remember climbing into bed. He didn't remember getting undressed. *Buddy?* His eyes opened in a flash. He sat up almost as fast and looked around. Where was Buddy?

He climbed out of bed and saw his clothes in a bunch on the floor. Buddy was half-tangled in them. His eyes were bugging out. There was his suit tie, partly hanging out of the side of Buddy's mouth. The bio-pet had tried eating it and was suffocating! Albert fell on the dying little animal and struggled to pull the tie out of his throat! Buddy struggled feebly. In death spasms, he was still trying to finish swallowing the tie. Albert quickly shoved his fingers in Buddy's mouth, forcing it open. He was bitten once and then Buddy relaxed. Albert pulled hard, and the tie came free and out of the motionless animal's mouth. "Buddy," he cried several times, wondering if he should attempt CPR. *Can you do CPR to a chicken-sized cartoon version of a T-rex?*

Buddy twitched just then and took a small breath. 'Buddy?" Albert ventured hopefully. His pet took another shallow breath. In a few moments, Buddy was trying to get up. Albert gathered the animal up into his arms and hugged it.

'Buddy has never tried eating a tie,' Albert wondered anxiously. Then he realized that he'd forgotten to feed Buddy dinner the night before. There was no breakfast put out either. The poor little guy must have been starving. Good thing he'd had the sudden urge to check on Buddy. The Time mail! The time mail had saved Buddy's life! Albert really loved time mail.

Albert lay on the sofa all day recovering from the late night and played with his pet. His eyeglasses rang. It was somebody out of his past. Allison! He had loved her, and then she'd broken his heart. That was two years ago. He didn't want to answer. He had gotten over her. The wound had healed.

He answered anyway. "Hello?"

"Albert?"

"Yes."

"I miss you."

Albert's heart ached. He held Buddy tight. "I miss you too."

"I want to see you."

Albert's voice caught in his throat. "I, I don't know."

There was silence for a while. "I understand. Bye," and she hung up with a tear in her voice.

Albert sat there holding Buddy for a long time. Two days later, he received a time mail. "CALL ALLISON ITS OK". At the bottom, as always, was the company logo. "Wasn't Tomorrow Wonderful!"

The End

You've got time-mail!

FROM: Me ⬍ TO: Me ⬍

DATE: One month in the future ⬍

The winning lottery number is 10 09 50 62 42

Reply to the ○ Future or the ○ Past

Message:

[Reset] [Submit]

1 Message, 0 unread, 1 t-mail is available to send

Wasn't Tomorrow Wonderful!

© Temporal Industries

Becoming Obsolete

"God, it's hot out," a stocky built man mumbled grumpily while wiping the sweat from the back of his neck. It was the fall and not supposed to be this hot. It felt like July. He hated July. The A/C was on in the office, but he wasn't allowed to be in there unless he had a customer. Lewis was a crook of the ordinary variety. He had no real friends. He had a dingy apartment in the "affordable" part of the city. It was filled with hand-me-downs from his mother's apartment. The expensive things like his TV were stolen. Lewis had a job at a used car lot and an ex-girlfriend with a young son he never saw. He paid child support when she could get his wages garnished. That was when it was time to dodge to a new job. He was surprised like everybody else when the wild rumor turned out to be true. He didn't pay it much mind. Then one day, his life crashed down upon his head.

The story about time mail had leapt from the conspiracy blogs to the headline news. A new website had opened without fanfare claiming to offer an email service with an amazing twist. You could talk to yourself exactly one month in the future or one month in the past.

The lot was as quiet as a desert. It was too hot and dirty out for most people to shop for a car. Lewis walked back into the small seedy show room. He kept an eye out for his boss. It was much cooler inside. There was a TV facing the empty chairs where customers would wait for a salesman. He listened to part of an interview while hoping that the receptionist in her low cut blouse would bend over a second time. The head of the Internet company was boasting about the service and the technology behind it. The enthusiastic man in the expensive suit chattered something about wiggling atoms with one displaced in time. God, but the receptionist was smoking. The TV droned about wiggling one atom causing the other to wiggle a month earlier. There was another statement about looking at atoms without really looking at them. Somewhere in Lewis's sluggish brain, he formed the thought, "wasn't that something." But what good was a month? If he could talk across three years then he could warn himself that that bitch Mindy was skipping her pill and he'd have known to dump her before she got pregnant.

Lewis didn't notice it right away when things had started to really go wrong. He had fewer customers, but there had always been dry spells. Maybe he had fallen off his game? No. It was the awful heat. It got hotter every summer, but people always sooner or later needed a car. Like a crocodile lurking in a swamp, he could wait. He was only half conscious that he hadn't sold a junker in the last month. It couldn't be him. It had to be the heat. Yet, his boss Monkey Joe in that gaudy three piece suit was making more jabs at him than usual. Hmmm… Maybe it was that Lemon-buster app people could download to their smart eyeglasses. He'd heard about it. One look at the VIN number on the dashboard and the buyer had all of the dirt on the car's history displayed in their smart eyeglasses. Yep. That must be it. He'd have to doctor the VIN numbers on the junkers.

Lewis didn't call his boss, Monkey Joe to his face. Joe thought he was so important because he wore that monkey suit. One day Lewis would steal and burn that three piece business suit. He smiled at the mental image of Monkey Joe's devastation and despair.

The junkers were the dealership's bread and butter. More and more of his sales were only the good cars and the dopes haggled less. His commissions were down. He hadn't made a killer deal in a couple of weeks. He hardly fought with angry customers trying to get their money back anymore either. Shame. It made Lewis happy to see grown men and women cry.

It was lunchtime break when it happened. One moment he was joking with the curvy receptionist and the next, his boss in his three piece business suit was marching out of the office all angry and fired him. That bastard! Joe had actually accused him of stealing! Sure, he'd done it before, but this time he hadn't. Monkey man was all pissy because he thought Lewis was going to steal some car batteries next Tuesday! They yelled at each other for a while, then Lewis stomped off to get his stuff. On the way out he got the tire iron from the trunk of his car so he could beat up Monkey Joe's BMW. But there was Joe. He was leaning up against his car, holding a baseball bat. Joe was wearing a big knowing grin. Then it struck Lewis like a big bag of cold ice hard in the face. Of course Joe knew Lewis was going to beat his car. Joe had gotten himself time mail!

Lewis was as angry as angry gets. Driving home, he ranted and raved. He banged the steering wheel and stomped his feet. He barely knew what he was doing and ran three red lights before he calmed down enough to drive safely. Then he became quiet and depressed. "Just great," he whined . He was unemployed again. But Lewis was resilient if anything. Most adults have a fall back position when times get hard. For most, it was the job when they did as a teenager. Some people get a part time job at a hardware store. Some deliver pizzas. Lewis was a thug and when times got tough he would resort to petty crimes. He always liked to refer to crimes as his, "second job".

The next day Lewis ate breakfast, then drank all morning. By evening, he was sobering up and cabin fever chased him out of his small cramped apartment. Walking down the streets of the big city, he was angry and depressed. There was one thing that always lightened his mood when he was like that. He took a bus to another part of town. On the way, he had become giddy with excitement.

This park was new to him, but they were all pretty much the same. He walked the grounds twice to scope out the place. It looked good. There was plenty of cover and exits. It'd been a while. He'd break the ice with a simple purse snatch and grab. Maybe even a juicy mugging if the dope was frail. He liked the park so Lewis waited in the park, sizing up the people as they walked by. It was like fishing. Most were lost in the augmented reality of their smart eyeglasses. Some were playing games as they sat or walked, oblivious to everything going on around them. Some were chatting with friends. Others were watching TV or listening to audiobooks as they enjoyed the small patch of nature. To all, he was invisible. He loved it.

After a while, Lewis became frustrated. Something was wrong. None of the dopes he liked would pass near him. It was as if he was in a bubble. If he got too close, the dope would walk away changing speed to keep their distance. He swore that he even got a dirty look from one woman. She clutched her purse close to her chest when she saw him. She suddenly looked frightened and turned and quickly left the way she'd come.

Odd. Maybe he had dated her once? An hour passed with nobody coming close to him other than a homeless man. Then another passed. He'd received two more glares before it was obvious the fish weren't biting today. He left in a sour mood.

Not perturbed, Lewis broke out his own pair of smart eye glasses once he got home. They were in a drawer in his bedroom. He didn't use them very often. He thought that eyeglasses detracted from his rugged handsomeness. He already had the "Nobody's Home" app installed in the augmented reality eyeglasses. The data was pulled from a website that gleaned data from social networking pages determining who was on vacation and who was not. It had been meant to make people socially aware, but instead became a boon for burglars. As the story goes, it had been shut down for moral reasons only to be reopened under a new name. He had heard that it was now owned by the Russian mafia, but who knew for sure?

He had a 3D printer connected to his computer. Both were stolen of course. He hadn't used it in a while so he was slow to figure out what to press. He rummaged through his computer for the copy of, "The Gangster's Handbook," that he had downloaded years back.

The e-book talked about what crimes were more profitable than others and how most criminals got themselves caught. He had once skimmed the words. He figured he knew more than the book about getting away with crimes. He was smarter than most people! He only had a copy for the data files it contained. The tools he could make were pretty useful.

Using the 3D printer, he printed lock pick tools and a nasty knife. The gun he had to ponder over. When the menu asked him what type of ammo he had, Lewis had to dig through several drawers before finding some sad looking twenty two caliber shorts. There were only three bullets. That was OK. He wasn't going to kill anybody unless he was surprised. Cops would try harder to get you if you killed somebody.

When he entered this information into the computer, the Gangster's Handbook scaled the barrel thickness down to the weaker ammunition. It then asked if the pistol was to be an automatic with a clip, a revolver or a simple zip-gun. It cautioned that for the automatic, there would be extra assembly by hand and springs required. "Click here for the specification on the springs." The printer didn't make parts like powerful springs. It could only make weak ones.

Lewis skipped past the automatic and looked at the revolver. It had fewer parts to assemble. It also recommended test firing on a shooting range before relying on it in an actual shoot out. This looked like too much work. All he was planning was a simple burglary. He didn't expect to get into a gun battle.

The last category was zip guns. They had almost no parts and could use heavy rubber bands instead of springs. One was a two shot derringer style. The simplicity of the two shot gun had an Old West look that he found appealing. A couple of clicks later and the plastic gun started forming in the printer's "oven".

Lewis certainly wasn't the smartest man in the room, but he knew that there were molecular level serial numbers in the plastic liquid used by the 3D printer. It was there to catch crooks. So, he had stolen a supply of 3D ink when he'd stolen the computer.

It took several hours, but finally, he felt properly equipped. At eleven o'clock he left his apartment and strode into the night with the eagerness of a hunter. It was another half hour before the public transit system had him across the city. Fondling the plastic lock pick in his pocket, Lewis spent the late hours walking up and down the streets of two neighborhoods he'd never been in before. Occasionally his eyeglasses displayed a bubble superimposed on an apartment window. Every time one looked like a juicy candidate, a closer look proved somebody was home. Once there was a man sitting on the supposedly empty balcony, quietly in the dark. A light would go on once in a while or he'd see a face plastered against a window glass staring out onto the street. By three A.M., he gave up and dragged his weary soul home.

The next night found Lewis having a few beers in one of the neighborhood bars. His favorite show, "Cooking with Guns," was on. The man next to him was more of a business associate rather than a friend. But he had no real friends and really had no understanding of what a true friend was. Lewis half ignored Joey's whining about his mother, hooker girlfriend and life in general. It was a typical man's conversation.

He'd seen the TV episode before. It was the one where the Angry Chef used a shotgun to shoot the melons to make fruit salad. He wrapped various foods in aluminum foil and strapped them to his engine and tail pipe. The Chef then climbed into his car and drove across town, heckling the traffic and tried to pick up women by shouting out of the car window. In general he made a nuisance of himself while the food cooked. The thought that the obnoxious behavior might be an act and not the chef's real personality never occurred to Lewis. In general, he took the world at face value.

In the end, the Chef pulled up to the back of his restaurant and retrieved the food from the various locations across his car. In the kitchen, he carefully unwrapped each one, made it look pretty and served the gourmet meal to an unsuspecting couple. He always liked how the Chef would end the show on a bar stool, cigarette hanging out of a half open hand, resting on his knee and told everybody to go home because he had to wash the dishes.

The Angry Chef was a real salt of the Earth sort of guy. Lewis found the show very creative. He admired creative people. Lewis also found "Cooking with Guns" to be educational. He hadn't known that waiters didn't share their tips with the cook. The Chef bitched about it in almost half of the episodes. He agreed. It didn't seem right. You had a great meal and you tip the guy who walked across a room but not the guy who did the real work? That wasn't right.

He couldn't hear what the Angry Chef was saying over the crowd noise but he could hear his sometime associate. "I'm telling you," the man next to him speculated. "I haven't rolled anybody in a week because of that time mail thing. I figure that afterwards they rat me out to themselves so they know I'm coming long before I do! That ain't sporting. I chase and chase but can't catch anybody. It's just not right."

Lewis frowned into his cheap beer and remembered when he was little, playing tag with his big brother. No matter how he tried to touch his brother, Dave was always able to dodge out of the way.

Then it dawned on him. If the dopes could see the future then why couldn't he? It was a great idea! It was an idea too great to share. He was too excited to finish his beer. Without a word, he paid his tab and walked out of the bar, lost in deep thought.

Lewis wasn't as computer savvy as a ten year old. Yes, he played computer games growing up and occasionally bought something online but was otherwise uninterested in the net. So it took him a little while to find the time-mail site and fumble through getting an account. Finally, the time-mail website was there in all of its multi-media glory. A video of HG Wells climbing into his time machine and rushing into the future obscured where Lewis was supposed to click to create an account.

He clicked "yes" to the Terms of Use with a chuckle. He hadn't read the text, but knew it said that he wasn't supposed to use the time-mail for anything illegal. Funny. Like a little check box could keep him from doing what he wanted.

It wasn't long before he had his account and his inbox flashed at him with a catchy sound. Two emails! The first was a welcome from the company. The second was from himself? The spelling was poor, so the chances were that it probably was. There in black and white was tomorrow's winning lottery number! It was hard to believe, but there it was. He had sent it to himself from one month in the future!

Excitedly, Lewis rushed to the liqueur store arriving just before it closed. The annoyed clerk made a face when Lewis bought a single ticket with his special number. It didn't matter because tomorrow night he'd be rich!

He knew it would work because the scientist on TV had said so. You can change the past because at the quantum level, cause and effect can happen in the wrong order. He wasn't clear what that meant, but it was said on a News show so it must be true.

He was alone in his little apartment the next evening. As the time email promised, the lottery number was picked during his dinner of pizza and beer. He re-read this ticket three times before doing a dance, then read it twice more to be sure. Unbelievable! He had just won mega millions!

It was a week before the winnings were calculated and the money transferred from the lottery commission to his bank account. A whole lot of people had won the lottery. It was several million people, according to the news. Lewis' double checked his bank statement in disbelief. His share of the winnings was three dollars and twenty cents! The lottery ticket had cost more! How can an honest crook make a living anymore!

Over the next few months, time mail was all the press talked about. The news went on to say that because people could now tell the future, lotteries were obsolete. State governments were in a panic over the lost revenue. Casinos worldwide were all in danger of closing down. Insurance companies lost most of their travel insurance business.

Weeks went by. The world was going crazy. All the news talked about anymore was T-mail, T-mail, T-mail. The stock market was erratic due to brokers buying and selling a month earlier than before. An assassination of the CEO of Temporal industries was foiled. There was a failed bombing attempt of the T-Mail server farm. Congress was debating a bill restricting T-mail to one month into the future in response to the announcement that version 2.0 would extend to talking two months across time.

Meanwhile, Lewis suffered. He couldn't find a job. Mainly, he didn't get responses to his résumés he'd uploaded to various websites. When he did get an interview, the prospective employer would check their computer, frown and tell Lewis, "no thanks." Damn that T-mail!

Out of desperation, Lewis even tried to rob a grocery store and a liqueur store in one night! Both times, the police were lingering in numbers. Then there was the bank job. He'd gotten word of the money delivery too late to go after it himself. Luckily so, because the next day the breaking news was of camera footage of three and four man teams going into the bank every fifteen minutes or so, only to be pounced on by the waiting army of police inside! The other interesting news piece on TV was about the court ruling disallowing anybody arrested of a crime or their lawyers to use T-mail. Felons couldn't vote, own a gun or use T-mail! Anybody giving a crook a heads up using T-mail would be arrested as an accessory. The ACLU was suing for freedom of speech. How could a man make a living in a world like this?

Over time the Stock market stabilized. With everybody looking a month into the future, it had become the same old thing. Just, the surprises were farther into the future.

Where the CNN future crime report and the Weather Channel were a raging success, organized sports teams started to fail. Nobody wanted to know who won or lost in advance.

Being unemployed for nearly a year had been a sobering experience for Lewis. He finally got a job in a grocery store and learned to keep his nose clean. He couldn't afford to lose this job or he'd be living on the sidewalk in a week. He didn't want that. As much as he hated it, he did use T-mail himself once in a while. It was mainly to find his lost keys.

The world began to settle down into a new pace. Lotteries learned not to announce the winners until over a month after being picked. State & Federal legislation was finally signed, barring civilian organizations from creating a time-mail that reached further than one month. Forced into the habit of being honest, Lewis even got himself a girlfriend. He secretly checked his T-mail every week for warnings about her. He suspected she did the same. All in all, life was working again.

But in the back of his mind, he just knew there must be a loophole. Day after day while stocking the shelves and sorting the fruit, he worked on the puzzle. If he could figure out how to beat T-mail, he'd be on top again. What could he steal that nobody would notice for longer than a month?

The End

Home | View | Contact us

You've got time-mail!

FROM: Me ⬍ , TO: Me ⬍

DATE: One month in the future ⬍

Cities are burning. Millions dead.

Reply to the ○ Future or the ○ Past

Message:

[Reset] [Submit]

1 Message, 0 unread, 1 t-mail is available to send

Wasn't Tomorrow Wonderful!

© Temporal Industries

The Arms Race in Time

Of the two hundred and eleven countries in the world, four were saber rattling at the United States. Fourteen were threatening each other. Five small regional wars were raging. The United States was not currently involved in armed combat. That didn't mean that it wasn't under siege.

The typical nation state endures an average of one hundred thousand cyber attacks a day. Spying and warfare over the Internet had become as common place as buying an e-book. Most small countries had mastered it as well as the large. It was a very cost effective way to project military power around the globe. As is the way of war, a new paradigm unexpectedly emerged. Whoever mastered it first would be the next superpower.

A military officer stood at a podium in a small briefing room in the Pentagon. In the audience was the President, the Vice President, the DNI and other leaders. The slide on the large screen changed. The briefer used a laser pointer to indicate different parts of the diagram as he talked. "What was built is a variation of the old Steven Hawking's Time machine concept. He proposed taking a wormhole and attaching one end to the Earth and the other to a spaceship. The spaceship would then travel away from Earth near the speed of light and return to Earth some time later. The end of the wormhole attached to the spaceship would experience time dilation, forcing it to exist in the past relative to the other end that had stayed on Earth"

A new diagram appeared. "Resulting in a time tunnel of a sort with the two ends a fixed time distance apart. For argument's sake, let's say it is one month. Toss an object in one end and it exits out the other a month later. But toss it in the opposite end and the object will exit the wormhole a month in the past."

The audience rustled at that. "Of course we don't know how to make a space-time wormhole or a build spacecraft that can go near light speed. So ten years ago the company now called Temporal Industries started a secret project to attempt to build the next best thing out of what our science can do."

"A Hawking's time machine requires two key elements. One is near light speed travel for an extended period of time. The other is to be able to travel instantaneously over a distance. Temporal Industries realized that every day, particle accelerators around the world commonly fling atoms at near light speed. They knew that at the atomic level, there is a long known curious phenomenon that allows information to be transmitted instantaneously, over long distances kind of like a wormhole would do for an object."

"What is this curious phenomenon? Einstein and Bohr in 1930 started an argument about the fledgling science of quantum physics. Einstein argued that special relativity was the truth and the Bohr's standard model was wrong because it allowed instant communication between entangled atomic particles. Entanglement is when two different particles think they are the same, single particle. However, Einstein was wrong. Entanglement turned out to be real. The first successful case of entangling photons in the lab was achieved in the 1990's. The first experiment successfully transmitting information was in 2011. Since then the technology has evolved into what we have today."

The President cleared his voice, announcing an interruption. "Is it true that Temporal Industries had approached the Department of Defense with this idea and we refused to fund them?"

The officer behind the podium in turn cleared his throat nervously. "Yes, Mr. President. At the time it must have sounded like a very ridiculous contract proposal."

"And now talking through time is available to everybody over the Internet, even terrorists, criminals and countries hostile to the United States of America."

"Yes, Mr. President."

The President looked back and forth at the Security Counsel members in the seats around him. He wished it was a hoax, but knew it wasn't. "What are our options?"

One of the Generals spoke up first. "We can evoke the Emergency Powers Act and declare the time email service as a threat to national security. We publicly announce we are shutting it down, but instead make it a DoD black project. We'd pay off, employ or imprison the scientists who have the key knowledge."

The science advisor spoke next. "It wouldn't work. The genie is out of the bottle. You can't uninvent anything. Now that everybody knows it can be done, those with enough resources can deduce and develop the remaining pieces to make their own time mail. At best we will have a ten year advantage. That's about how long it took the Soviets to build their first atom bomb."

The President perked up, "We have to quickly get in front of this problem and control the narrative. Can we use the time mail to send ourselves a warning, so we would shut this all down before it could go public?"

The science advisor shook his head. "No, Mr. President. You can only send the message back exactly 30 days into the past. You can't send it back any sooner than before the existence of the time machine. If I opened an account today, today would be the earliest I can receive a warning from the future." The irony was not lost on anybody in the room. They had a time machine, but couldn't use it to solve their time travel problem.

The General spoke up again, "We can only go forward with this problem which means containment! We grab control and lock everybody else out. Only we get to use it. Otherwise, we'll never have the element of surprise in combat again!"

"International trade deals of all manner could be stolen from us as other countries cheat and alert themselves about what the winning trade deals would have been," the Director of National Intelligence added. The realization sank in of how badly this could damage the economy.

"Mr. President," the Vice President interrupted. "It has been only two weeks and the public are embracing time-mail. Nay, they are becoming dependent on time-mail faster than any other technology in history. People are not only quickly learning how to use it to run their own lives better, they will very soon be utterly dependent on it. Imagine if we suddenly took away the public's cell phones, air conditioning, GPS, television or Internet. How would they react? Imagine if we took away their electricity! What if we banned religion! We'd risk serious civil uprising. We'd all be voted out of office and replaced with politicians that would give back to the people their temporal heroin."

The room broke out into a jumble of frustrated arguments. The President looked at the VP. He then announced loudly, "How do we contain the problem without taking it away from the public?"

The silence was finally broken by the Director of National Intelligence. "Mr. President. Gentlemen and gentlewomen. I respectfully think the challenge before us is not how to contain, but turn this situation to our advantage. I believe I know how." He then offered the outline of his plan. What intelligence agency would become the nation's advanced scouts in the future wasn't immediately obvious. It could be the Department of Homeland Security, CIA or any one of a long list of candidates. That was a minor detail to be worked out later. With no better idea in the room, the President gave his approval.

As with all great things, it started with a single team. Each wanting to control possibly the most powerful weapon in history, a compromise was reached. The team would be comprised of sixteen military billets with civilian leadership. Two of the billets were reserved for the Army. Likewise, the Air Force, Navy and Marines each had two permanent positions. Since time mail was accessed through the Internet, Cyber Command was tasked to manage the team.

Inside one of the many buildings that comprised the Command's headquarters was a 24 hour watch room with dozens of workstations built into wide desks arranged in two concentric arcs. This was where the nation's top cyber defenders sat. They had global awareness and global reach. On the Wall in front of them were several large video screens that wrapped a third of the way around a circular room. The screens showed the status of the Internet and tactical information whenever there was a crisis. When a crippling Internet virus was released, the growing infection was shown spreading on many real-time maps. Most nations had similar rooms with similarly qualified defenders and attackers.

Being the hot new thing, Congressmen were demanding tours through the watch room on a daily basis. The constant interruptions were making it hard for the for military duty officers to focus on the tasks of inventing their job duties. It also was a distraction to cyber warriors who suddenly weren't the special kids anymore. Everybody wanted to feel like they were a piece of the action. They all wanted to be a part of this historic moment.

It was easy for Congress to invent the job of Time Defender. It was an altogether different problem determining specifically what somebody sitting at a workstation all day would actually do. Task number one was to put a sign on the four desks that called them Time Defenders. Quickly and efficiently, it was completed! "Time Defenders" sounded campy and had lots of syllables. So, the young men and women were referred to in the plural, TDs.

Task two was to assign the young TDs to the various shifts which was quickly completed. Task three was for each to create two user accounts on the time mail website. This was a problem. Net congestion and server timeouts made getting onto the website a frustrating hell. There were far too many people across the world also trying to get on it at the same time. They were all stepping on each other. The time mail web servers teetered on collapse.

The team's goal was to use different aliases for each account to help hide from cyber warriors from other countries. It was so difficult getting onto the website long enough to accomplish this that after a week only one account had been created. Still, it was a success. In 30 days, they would be able to send warnings back through time. Immediately, their future selves could warn their present selves about of any future attacks on the Nation.

When the operator accessed his inbox an hour and a half later, there was mail. They had received their first message from the future! It read, "FINISH BOOK ASAP". The message must mean the codebook. Impatient future people. And that was it. There wouldn't be another message until sometime the next day.

The two men and two women would spend most of their shift settling into their brand new jobs while they occasionally tried and retried to open the require t-mail accounts. They filled out HR forms and took mandatory online training. Some of the classes were on how to write action reports. Most were mandatory classes on all manner of subjects such as prevention of sexual harassment and how to put classification markings on a document. Beyond that, there was not much to do. They were inventing the job out of thin air. It didn't need eight men to check sixteen accounts every hour. Boredom was going to be a big part of their life. The soldiers didn't mind. In boot camp it had been beaten into them that being a soldier was to experience long periods of boredom broken by short periods of extreme terror and violence.

They started the creation of a theoretical tool kit. It would consist of plausible ways time can be used.

If there was nothing in one t-mail account, why would there be something in the other? They could create new accounts if they needed them.

Messages were limited to twenty characters, all caps. How to maximize the amount of information one can squeeze into twenty letters?

Careers were going to be built and quickly. Whatever they did, they were making history. Several levels of management above the action team all anxiously wanted to take part in the excitement. They used their authority to reach down and micromanage the defender's along with their immediate management, the Director of Time and his technical director. Since the government loves acronyms, they were referred to the DT and the TD.

As the mission operators were TDs, confusion abounded.

The Technical Director, Andrew Buckley shook his head, "No. The first character in all time messages should tell which code book to refer to." The four others in the room thought about it then agreed. What the rest of the letters in the time messages would do would be harder to determine. They would be used to signify what word or phrase in the code book to pick. A sequence of these references would build the entire message.

This would serve two purposes, if discovered and read by a hostile foreign cyber warrior, the enemy would get an unreadable random sequence of letters. It was an idea that went back thousands of years. The other and more important purpose was to allow much more information to be sent in a single message. It would be hard to warn yourself that, "The Japanese were going to bomb Pearl Harbor on Sunday, December 17, 1941 using a carrier fleet and mini submarines. They will be coming from..." in twenty capital letters a day or less! But if a code book had one letter that represented which country in a look up table was to attack them, the next letter was the type of attack, the third letter represented the day, month, and so on, it was possible to squeeze a huge amount of information into twenty letters. All they had to do was agree on the scheme of the code book and fill it in with all of the information they predicted they might want to tell themselves.

The team was feeling very anxious. Creating anything by committee always took forever and their future selves, 30 days from now were clearly unhappy. This straight forward task must not go well. In a month they obviously needed the codebook ASAP. Until they got the job done, they could only understand brief messages, written in the clear, messages that their adversaries could also read.

Three days later the Time Defenders with their lone account received a message stating, "BOMBING OF TIME MAIL". They sent out an alert to the Department of Homeland Security and the FBI. By week's end, a truck bomb was found in the parking ramp under the headquarters of Temporal Industries. The driver was apprehended before he could escape and the bomb was diffused. It was the team's first major success. It also made them worry about the value of the actual time travel facility out side of Chicago.

Andrew was invited to attend the FBI briefing to the National Security Counsel in the War room at the Pentagon. He was there in case there were any questions about his team. "This was clearly a lone wolf operation. Domestic Terrorism," the Special Agent explained. "There were two men and one woman who made the truck bomb out of materials any farm would have. We found no evidence of a larger conspiracy. Their motive was to stop time mail."

"Islamic?" the President asked.

"No. It is a small, obscure new age cult with paramilitary rhetoric, powered by a paranoia of the Federal Government. Basically, Satan is an alien who works his evil by controlling the CEO of Temporal Industries who in turn is giving god-like powers to the Federal Government to enslave all people for all time."

There was a quiet rumbling in the audience. They didn't know what to think. It was too strange. The speaker continued, "Blowing up the office building in Chicago would not have achieved their goal. The building only contained business offices. Clearly there is a need to provide serious protection of the time machine and server rooms in Utah. We also need to increase protection of the old Fermi National accelerator. It is the mothballed particle accelerator Temporal Industries purchased twelve years ago. It is what they use to unstuck in time the two ends of the quantum particles. These particles don't last and must be continuously replaced."

One of the five star generals spoke up, "We can have the national guard secure both facilities in twenty four hours! That'll give the army time to build a permanent perimeter. We'll bring in mobile anti-ballistic missile launchers." The man gleefully savored the prospect of heavy military machinery lumbering across the countryside and take an active defensive position against an imagined determined enemy.

"We'll have to declare the air space above both facilities as no-fly zones," another general interrupted. He couldn't let the first man take all the glory for defining the defenses. These early days not only were going to define many careers but some of them would surely end up in the history books!

"And defend Temporal Industries computer networks," Andrew thought to himself. He didn't dare to speak up. He was politically less than nothing to this group of men and women. If they didn't come up with it themselves, he'd pass the thought on to Cyber Command when he got back to the office.

"Gentlemen," the President interrupted. "We can't grab control of a major business from the hands of its citizens. The Public won't stand for it."

The Generals looked flustered. They knew better than to blurt out anything to their commander and chief without first running it through their heads a couple of times. The Director of National Intelligence took advantage of the pause to inject his own ideas. "We won't have to. We'll merely make Temporal Industries run like a proper Defense Contractor. We'll declare the key facilities as classified work places. We'll require the company to adhere to DoD security standards. The FBI will run background checks on the employees at the facilities. We'll hold their hands through the process so they don't feel too overwhelmed." There were nods of approvals all around.

"And we'll still deploy tanks and anti-ballistic missile batteries around their perimeter," the Army General quickly added.

"And close the airspace," the Air Force General followed quickly.

Over the next couple of weeks Temporal industries was helped to better protect its buildings. The network problems subsided and the Time Defender's succeeded in creating all of the accounts they needed.

In the desks next to them, the Cyber Warriors guarded the networks they used. Other agencies hunted for Terrorists, Criminals and foreign governments using time mail and those seeking out their own accounts to spy on.

The Time Defenders received daily messages from the future. None were classified. Each were statements about articles in the news. Occasionally there was an action about a school shooting or a horrible accident. These were no doubt also being reported back through time by the police and the families of the injured. As far as Andrew knew, the government wasn't running into save the day, but the politicians wanted to claim that his team was regularly thwarting disasters. The new normal was beginning to settle in.

The reports they were writing were not matters of national security but politically chosen. This annoyed the team, but it did serve a useful purpose. It allowed them to practice their jobs over and over so they could respond quickly when a real emergency occurred. It uncovered a flaw in their strategy. The team had learned a new trick. A new lesson. They had a new tool for their Time Defender's toolkit. They should send the individual messages back at different times throughout the day. Their response time to an emergency would be faster if they used a staggered schedule.

The reports from the Time Defenders thirty days in the future continued to arrive daily. There was no sign of major trouble. There were always worries and saber rattling between foreign countries. With so many having nuclear bombs, they rarely did more than bark at each other. Time-mail had everybody's society was in turmoil.

A major cyber attack from an unknown party locked out Internet access to the time mail. It was a massive denial of service attack. It lasted for four days before Cyber Command was able to neutralize it. They didn't know who had done it. Various hacker groups blamed each other then started a cyber attack war on each other. Time-mail got hit a few more times. Cyber command quickly protected it. The various hack-activist groups weren't as sophisticated as many of the governments around the world.

There was a warning about a plan to assassinate of the CEO of Temporal Industries. The FBI was investigated and neutralized the threat.

Several politicians, including the President were under fire for using time mail to send incriminating dirt about their opponents backwards to themselves to help their party win the past and upcoming elections. There was blood in the water. The team was keeping far away from any mud Congress was throwing at each other.

Work of the codebook continued to go poorly. It was strangled by the bureaucracy. The more upper managers tried to help, the more the work got twisted horribly forcing them to start the effort over. Meanwhile, the TDs made do in their t-mails with abbreviated English.

Andrew was discussing an issue with one of his team when he was waved to by his boss and another man through the glass window of one of the briefing rooms connected to the watch room. "I'll be right back."

He strolled up the stairs, opened the door to the glass room and walked inside. "What's up?"

"This is Randall Hofstadter of the CIA. Not his real name. This is Andrew Barkley, my technical director. Please repeat to him what you told us?"

"We have reason to believe that there is a threat to the nation." Andrew was completely focused on Mr. Hostadter. We received a warning from the future. We have our own agents with t-mail accounts. Don't look surprised. Nearly everybody in the world has an account by now."

Of course. Andrew and his wife had their own personal accounts. "What is the threat and when will it happen?"

"The message was cryptic then the agent when silent. Actually, all of our agents went silent."

"Where are your future agents?"

"The far future."

Andrew looked surprised. This wasn't what he expected to hear. He had expected a where not a when. The far future? "But how?'

The man from CIA shook his head, "Sorry. Classified."

"From how far in the future?"

"Five months. Maybe more."

Andrew's mind started buzzing. How did they do that? They couldn't have created another time machine so fast. Did they somehow already have one? Could they have found a way to trick out time mail? "And you want to talk to us about what?"

"We don't know what the message means. We want your help. The more eyes on it the better. The message stated, "!ARMS RACE IN TIME!" It was surrounded by exclamation points. One explanation for how all of our are agents being silent is that communications to the future may have been cut off. We think something significant will happen, and quickly."

Arms race in time? "Isn't there already an arms race? We're likely building our own time machine. Other large countries must be also. Who builds one that reaches the furthest backwards will have an advantage."

Mr. Hostadter replied, "And when there is a second secret machine hidden somewhere, our public machine will be a target. Yes, but our analysts are puzzling over the message. Why send an obscure statement like this instead of actionable information? We think our future selves get a really nasty surprise. Somehow a panicky agent had a split second to send a warning. If it took too long to create a proper message, or he knew the message could be intercepted somehow, he'd send an obscure warning."

"Could the arms race turn into something else in the near future? What happened in past arms races?"

His boss shifted his weight from one foot to the other. "They generally go on for a long time. There is a lot of saber rattling. New technologies are invented. After a couple of decades, one side sometimes feels superior enough that they start a war. But everybody sees the war coming."

Mr. Hofstadter looked worried. "We've thought of that. Europe and China would fall into this scenario, but neither is expansionist. There'd be no need for a panicky message. Obviously, we are missing an important detail. There is something significant about this statement to our agent that isn't yet significant to us." The real worry was that history is replete with examples of big, powerful nations being surprised by the little guy being clever. Often, the little guy had been fatally clever. Could time itself be turned into a weapon? In World War one, it was a surprise when the first pilot of a fragile plane thought to carry a gun. Then somebody thought to toss a small bomb out of the cockpit while over enemy territory. It's always a surprise the first time.

The next few days were marathon meetings with military strategists. The problem and advantage of t-mail was the same. You couldn't surprise the other side because if they survived the first blow, they'd warn themselves. So the plan was, in the event of our side starting a war, time-mail would be turned off a month before the start of hostilities. This denied the enemy the ability to warn themselves. In a few years, when there were several time machines hidden around the world, this trick would become useless. By then whoever was able to reach the furthest backward in time would have the advantage.

So what if the adversary took out time-mail in the first strike? It seemed inconceivable to think of a military plan without time mail. And it had been only a couple of months. Until the other machines existed, the US had the advantage. Take it away? If the machine was destroyed, then nobody would have an advantage for at least a couple of years. Trip the lead runner so you have a chance to catch up.

It was four more months before there was the major outage. The administrators at Time Mail didn't know what had happened. "We're only getting random static from the machine. It appears that the whole machine has failed. It shouldn't happen. There is redundancy built into the design. There were thousands of independent data paths. It's spread across three separate power and network grids. Yet, there was no coherent information coming from the future. As best we could tell, we are still sending to the past."

"What could cause a total outage?"

"Well, the entanglement is fragile," the system administrator responded over the phone. "If the three independent containment systems failed, then all of the entanglement would break." The voice made a popping sound. "Like soap bubbles."

"The machine is completely broken?"

"Not completely. None of the entangled particles last forever. We lose individual pairs all of the time. That's why we keep making more with the accelerator. But losing them all at one moment. That would be bad. That would be really bad. We'd have a gap in service for at least a month, longer depending what happened to the containment vessels. Somebody is sure to get fired."

Andrew felt better. Just not a lot. He had a nagging feeling that whatever would happen in thirty days wouldn't be friendly.

The next morning when he woke up for work, his wife woke up also. "You had a rough night," she yawned. Andrew's was rubbing his sore neck. He was exhausted. The time mail outage had him a little anxious. "You tossed and turned all night." She rolled over, grabbing one of the long pillows to snuggle with. She didn't have to get up for work for another hour. "You kept talking in your sleep."

Andrew was in the bathroom lathering shaving cream on his face. "Oh yeah? Was it interesting?"

"No," Mary called back slurring with sleep in her voice. "Something about an arms race. You said it a lot."

Over the next two days passed, the time mail outage continued. The media was filled with speculation and conspiracy theories. The public was upset at their safety blanket being taken away. Time industries promised the outage was temporary.

Andrew's anxiety grew. It was clear. There must have been a quick and immediate failure of the future side of the time machine. In twenty seven days they'd know what had happened. They would experience it first hand. The TI technicians were preparing for major repairs, totally guessing what might be needed. The new particles would be stored at the accelerator until the future problem whatever it was, was solved.

Andrew and Mary were at their favorite happy hour. It was Wednesday, their regular midweek date night. Their young son was being watched by the neighbor, who was their regular sitter. Mary knew her husband was worried, but was smart enough not to press him about work. He wouldn't tell her no matter how she asked or complained. He'd been moody and distracted for days. It was getting worse. He was beginning to mumble.

Somebody from his past walked out of loud chattering crowd. "Andrew!" the man shouted.

Andrew could hardly hear him. He raised his glass. *Who was that guy?* He knew him from somewhere.

The man slapped Andrew on the back, "Long time no see! Who is this?" He asked, looking at Andrew's wife.

"Mary!" Andrew shouted back. How did anybody hold conversations in noisy bars, Andrew wondered. Mary Smiled at the stranger.

"I'm Peter! Great to meet you! Can I buy you two a beer? Oh yeah, you two already have one. I'll get the next round. Andrew, you still work for the government?"

Andrew nodded. His work may be classified, but the fact that he worked for the government wasn't. Peter. Peter. Oh yeah. Peter something. They had graduated college together. They had been in several classes. Been friends. It had been years since he had thought of Peter.

They drank and chatted for a while. Peter had signed up for a job in Antarctica. He was leaving in a week and would be gone for a year. Occasionally he'd look over his shoulder, searching the crowd.

"Looking for somebody?" Andrew asked.

"Naw," Peter shouted back. "Just looking to see if I recognized anybody else in the place." He paused. "I need a smoke, come outside with me?"

"OK," Andrew agreed. "Mary, I'll be right back."

Outside, Peter pulled out an electric cigarette. He turned it on and inhaled nicotine. Water vapor exited the fake cigarette giving the illusion of smoke.

His phone rang. "One sec," then into the phone, "Hello?"

Andrew stood there waiting. He slowly slid back into his worries. He was there for a while.

"Andrew? Andrew?" Peter was looking at him in concern. Andrew was suddenly aware he had been very deeply lost in thought. "Is something wrong? You were mumbling. You kept saying, Arms Race in Time."

Andrew stared quietly back, "Did I?"

"Are you OK?"

"I've had a rough day. And too much to drink."

"What about the book?"

Confused Andrew asked, "The book?"

Peter took a draw on his cigarette. "Yeah, the book. It took me a while to remember it."

"What book?"

"The Arms Race in Time."

A book? A book! "What do you remember about the book?"

Peter shrugged. "That was back in college. I bought a second hand copy at Good Will or somewhere. Maybe a yard sale. It was by a nobody author. Not a bad story though."

"I haven't read it. I might want to. What is the story about?"

"Let's see. It was a time travel story. There was a time machine made out of a wormhole. It was invented by that famous physicist in the wheelchair. You could send radio through it back and forth between the future and the past. It was a fixed distance in time like time-mail." Peter paused as he pondered the similarity to time mail. Interesting. If he could find a copy, maybe he'd read it again.

"And?"

"What? Oh. I think they talked to each other a year into the future. Oh. The hero figured out how to chain the time periods together so he could send a warning a couple years into the past. You know, to save the day, but it didn't work out very well."

"Chained together?"

"Andrew, you're pushing me. If you sent a message into the past asking the person in the past to send into the past..."

Could it be that simple? "Save the day from what?"

"A couple rogue countries, I don't remember which ones, teamed up to attack America. They smuggled a couple of nukes into the country and drove them around hidden in bread trucks. I think they were Los Angeles and Washington DC. The time machine was in LA, I think. The hero figures it out and gets the warning off just before the two cities explode. There was a big flash of light and the hero is killed. At the same time, war breaks out overseas. With the US out of the picture, the bad guys conquer the world. Then the message appears in the past warning everybody."

The next morning was twenty six days before the unknown. Andrew's mind was racing. We'd see ballistic missiles coming. But a nuke in a bread truck... That was so old school. "Twenty six," was all Andrew could say. He stared at Peter for another moment, then replied, "Thanks. You don't know how great it was to see you." Andrew then turned and ran into the parking lot and found his car. One hour to get to work! He didn't even think to tell his wife he had left until he was halfway to the office. She was angry when he called and told her to call a taxi.

Andrew walked into the watch room. The cyber warriors didn't notice him. They were fully engaged in monitoring and defending numerous pieces of the Internet. His night team stopped eating popcorn and watched him approach. Until now, he had been unhappy about there being so many of them with so little to do. That had all changed. Andrew showed three fingers to them, then pointed at the glass meeting room.

Once they were all in there he turned to one of the TDs, "We have an emergency. We need the boss." Andrew picked one of the soldiers, "You can't call him. Go to his house and bring him back, ASAP. Go!"

"The rest of you, we need to brain storm. How many t-mails do we have left to send tonight?"

The remaining two soldiers looked at each other, " Five," one replied.

"OK. That message the CIA had given us. It's a book title. An old book. It's about a time machine that's a lot like time-mail and a nuclear attack on two of our cities."

Stunned silence. "The t-mail outage?"

"It fits. A total failure could easily be one of the bombs going off near the machine in Utah. The other city in the book that got hit was DC. Apparently our military overseas also gets hit."

"A book?" Then the two thought about it. Why not? It wouldn't be the first time.

"We need to send a message back but it can't be in the clear. We have to assume the enemy is in our networks. Assume they have found our team and are monitoring our accounts. If they see us sending out a warning they may detonate the bombs now."

One of the soldiers raised his hand questioningly. Andrew continued. "It needs to be encrypted."

"But the code book isn't done."

"What codes we do have changes every week. A month ago, it would unencrypt wrong," replied the other.

Andrew shook his head. He had a plan. "For starters, we're going to send all the way back to when you all first arrived. No, it's true. The CIA said so. I know how it's done. It's in that book. It's so simple."

"But how?"

"Time Mail is basically a Hawking's machine. The idea is old. Somebody merely thought about it. Once you know, it is so obvious you want to smack yourself in the forehead for being so stupid. We haven't seen it because we thought the rules of how the machine worked were rigid. Back to the message. We need to maximize what we say in five, t-mails. It has to be obscured in a way that any of us can figure out. But it needs to look encrypted. The enemy would expect hard encryption so we might bluff our way through it."

"We need to break it up across all of the messages," one offered. They debated for an hour about how to do it.

"With the messages split into slices like shredded paper, there needed to be a clue how to put them back together."

"The first letter of each line would be in the first message. The second letter of each line would be in the second message, and so forth."

"We should have a clue what order the messages should be arranged. How about the first letter of each message being a sequence. One, two, three, four, five."

"Too obvious. How about letters. A, B, C, D and so on. The codebook is planned to use the first letter of the messages to tell us what version of the code book to use. If our messages get intercepted, they might think we have a lot of codebooks already done."

Andrew patted the woman on the back. "I like it. Now, if nobody has a better idea, let's figure out what we want to actually say. We have to do it in one hundred characters or less."

The day had changed. Midnight had passed before they were ready. This turned out to be to their advantage. They had sixteen t-mails to use in their message. The message could be three hundred and twenty characters long!

In twenty minutes the final message was done. The TDs opened all sixteen accounts and typed in the sixteen different messages. The text was triple checked and with a nod, they clicked send in each of the sixteen command windows.

That was it. They had alerted the past and the past had a month ago, alerted their past two months ago had alerted their past and on until the month their team of Time Defenders had started work in the watch room.

Nothing had changed. Did the past receive their warning? He had no memory of receiving the message every month since his job had started. He couldn't dwell on it now. They had to write up and send out the high priority alert, the Department of Homeland Security, National Security Counsel and the FBI. Everybody and more would be spun up in hours.

Before long that message was sent and there was nothing to do but worry, agonize and ponder. They were the men and women in the watch towers on the edge of their society. They had seen something bad approach and blown the horns warning the village. Now it was the job for those with guns, trained to protect who would run out into the woods and stop the threat. It was he and his people's job to stay in the towers and continue to watch. But the future was silent and would stay so for too long to make a difference. They had twenty five days before the unknown.

The team had learned a new trick. A new lesson. They had a new tool for their Time Defender's toolkit. The past can warn the past and on to the beginning of the time machine. Funny that they whom the public thought of as experts, as superheroes hadn't come up with this on their own.

The best theory was that each decision was a fork in the road between realities. If this was true than the world they had warned wasn't in the same reality than their own. Was the Andrew in the past a different person than the Andrew in the present?

These other people may have saved themselves a month ago. His reality has twenty five days to do the same if it can. Could it be that he had started a ripple across many realities? Many millions of people on many worlds may have just avoided a sudden flaming death. How could he ever know?

Screw it. Andrew had enough of the bureaucratic quagmire. He called two of his team over and told them to write their own unofficial codebook. They had until the end of their shift to have the outline of the structure. This they did. The next shift's task was to populate the code look-up tables with everything they may need to say based on their experiences to date, starting with the current emergency. They'd call it codebook Z. He'd given them two days to get it done. Something was better than nothing! Upper management didn't need to know about it. If it was a secret, they couldn't screw it up.

It was only two hours before Andrew was overwhelmed with having to answer a flood of questions about the alert they'd sent out and defend his belief. Not surprisingly, it had been received with skepticism. At least it hadn't been dismissed out of hand. Maybe he was crazy? Maybe he had jumped the gun? Over and over he was growled at, "So you think that one or more foreign governments might have one or more nukes in one or more of our cities in one or more trucks? There are hundreds of millions of trucks out there! You sure aren't giving us much to go on!" The next couple of days were painful.

Sixteen days left before the unknown. Andrew and his team had heard nothing about the hunt for foreign agents or terrorists. Maybe no news was a good thing? The FBI, CIA and the rest had no obligation to keep him appraised of their progress. Saying that a cheap novel from the past predicted an attack in their immediate future sounded rather ridiculous. Andrew didn't care as long as the hunt continued. If he was wrong, they'd fire him and he'd have to start his career over. If millions didn't die, he'd be Ok with that.

That night on his way home, he stopped at the store and bought a lot of canned food, water and first aid kits. Mary's concern over her husband's brooding behavior changed to alarm when he emptied his car, hauling load after load into their home. He wouldn't give her a reason beyond stating a few times, "You just never know."

Fourteen days left before the unknown. There was still no contact with the future. He had given up hoping that the outage was some fixable glitch. Without it, his team had nothing to send reports about except the occasional one to the past.

In sharp contrast to the dozens of always active men and women defending the nation from endless cyber attacks, the four Time Defenders sat quietly reading novels. The assignment his boss had handed them all was to seek out and read any piece of fiction that had a time travel plot that was plausible enough to inspire a real attack on the nation. They then would used those scenarios to sanity check their operating procedures. The first book of course had been, "The Arms Race in Time." It had been hard to find but there were still a couple copies out on the Internet. It was OK. It was a little dated, but OK. So far, everybody's favorite was Asimov's, "End of Eternity." Now there was a great plot! The insider threat element was food for thought. Two of the team were trying to adapt it to their type of time machine with the goal of identifying ways that time travel of information could be used against them.

Seven days before the unknown. No word on the hunt for the nukes. Was anybody still searching? His home was only a half hour drive from Washington DC. DC had to be a target. Andrew was doing a lousy job of trying not to panic. He hadn't had more than two hours of sleep a night in two weeks. His boss and team looked just as haggard. Out of desperation, he directed the team to send a new t-mail obscured in the same fashion as before. It asked if their past selves had received their warning that they had sent weeks ago? Had they understood it? Had they believed it? Nothing bad had happened when they'd sent the warning. It had to be safe to send a second one back asking if the first had made it.

When Andrew got home, he yelled at his wife to pack her bags and take their son to their Grandparent's home in Connecticut. They had to leave first thing in the morning. They weren't allowed to come back for two weeks. The yelling and crying went on for two hours, but the next morning, scared out of their wits, Mary and their young son raced off. The tires squealed. Their eyes overflowed with tears. Mary didn't know if her husband was insane or not. Maybe there really was some danger he wasn't allowed to tell her. At that moment it didn't matter. She was so upset that she never wanted to return.

When Andrew dragged himself into work, there was a message for him from the past. The four young soldiers had already pieced it together and read it. It was sent to them obscured using the same scheme. The, "A" t-mail had the first letters of each line. The "B" t-mail had the second letter of each line. "YES. WE RECEIVED , REPORTED AND PASSED THE WARNING BACK. EVERYBODY IS HUNTING. ANY LUCK IN THE FUTURE?"

At least somebody believed them. Then it occurred to him that he didn't remember ever sending such a message to the future. This meant that the people they were talking to in the past really weren't themselves after all! And they were having a conversation! The time machine didn't reach just backwards but across realities! He let that thought sink in for a moment. The physicists had said that one reality replaced the other. Could they be wrong? Could two realities coexist? They had to. This was important somehow. He just didn't know what it was. Were they talking across dimensions? Parallel universes? How could he ever tell? For a time wonder had replaced panic and despair.

Three days before the unknown. Mary and his son were in Connecticut. She wouldn't talk to him on the phone. Andrew stopped going home and had taken to sleeping in his office chair. He shaved in the men's room down the hall from the watch room. His boss at least still went home. The soldiers looked clean and neat. They were more afraid of their Captain than what might happen in a few days.

Andrew and his boss consulted then gave the team a message to obscure and send back. It read,

"WANTED TO SAY GOODBYE AND GOOD
LUCK IN YOUR REALITY IN CASE WE DON"T
FIND THE BOMBS IN TIME IN OURS"

It was early morning of the second day before
the unknown. Andrew woke up in his office chair to
a commotion. He smelled bad and he knew it. The
door to his office has flown open and his four young
men and women had burst in, excited and all
chattering at once.

"What?" He needed a cup of coffee badly.

"Messages! Sixteen messages!" was all he
could make out from the excited mob.

"What message?" Was the future back on
line? "From who?"

"It's a big one!" Andrew filtered out.

Andrew glanced at his watch. It was six A.M.
Two of the soldiers had produced electronic markers
and were writing letters on the large digital white
board that was one of the walls. "From the past?"

"Yes, sir! It's solid letters. No periods for
spaces like we have been using." It took two minutes
to get the slices written on the board, mistakes erased
and fixed.

They had to figure out where one word ended
and the next started. But wow. It read, "4 NUKES
LA DC NYNY UTAH STOLEN PLUMBR VANS"
and the addresses where they were found parked,
waiting to go off! There were four nukes, not two!
They were in plumber's vans or would be in a day or
two. And they knew where they'll be parked!

The team scrambled to send off the alerts to
the FBI and the rest. After weeks of boredom it was
suddenly very busy again. It wasn't twenty minutes

before Andrew, unshaven, grubby and all was dragged into marathon meetings to explain and repeat what had just happened.

The next day the team received a second set of sixteen t-mails. When pieced together they described attacks on several targets around the globe. Three countries were listed as behind the planned attacks.

On day zero, no cities were incinerated. Ten million people didn't die a horrible death. They continued to live, breath, love and toil as before. In a blink of an eye, the danger had invisibly passed.

The truck bombs had been found and quietly disarmed with hours to spare. They were big nukes, not the small ones that were used in World War II. Overseas, the three nations behind the truck bombs had planned simultaneous attacks on America's military forces. In one swift stroke both the head and the arms of the super power was to have received a knockout punch. The remaining countries, even the three remaining big ones like Europe and China were expected to be too surprised to intervene. Then they'd cower in indecision for fear that they could receive a similar fate. Delay would change to negotiation and a new world order would take shape.

The war didn't play out as planned. All of the attacks were supposed to have happened simultaneously. Not knowing their truck bombs hadn't gone off, devastating much of four states and irradiating dozens more, they launched their multi-pronged attack. In the three aggressor nations, ground based laser cannons shot beams of searing light up into the sky, blinding all of the US and European spy satellites across one hemisphere. Out in the Pacific, Guam's anti-missile defenses battled against a sudden wave of submarine launched aerial drones. The drones failed to get close enough to get off a single successful shot. Yet, Guam's defense parameter was penetrated by two of the first wave of hypersonic cruise missiles. They were armed with a fuel air burst technology. They devastated large areas by both their huge shock waves and temporarily eliminating most of the oxygen from the air. Most of the second wave made it through causing significant damage and loss of life across the island. Guam was defeated in less than an hour.

The Pacific and Mediterranean fleets faired much better. Being on high alert, they successfully fended off the worst of the surprise attack. Their point defenses intercepted most of the torpedoes and anti-ship missiles. Damage was light. More than the usual number of stealth fighters had already been in the air on no-notice practice maneuvers. At the time the pilots were surprised that the fighters were loaded with live ordinances. They reacted in the first minutes, sprinting at hypersonic speed to intercept the aggressors where they appeared.

Mini-fast robotic boats spread out from the fleets hunting mines and enemy submarines, most of which had been tracked for days by Navy hunter killer subs. As numerous as they were, the enemy submarine fleet didn't last much longer than their surface ships.

The Pacific and Mediterranean fleets paused for hours once the battle was over. They had held the field. Once they had regrouped and re-armed, they launched retaliatory strikes. The numerous scattered battles that ensued weren't easy. But in the end, all of three of the aggressor nation's major military facilities and defenses were in flames. The power stations feeding their cities were disabled. The war had lasted seventy eight hours.

Back in the watch room, Andrew and his team had learned a new trick. The past can save the future. The shifting waters of realities can save each other in both directions. In his car on the way home after a very long day, a thought occurred to Andrew. The first time mail they ever received, said to finish the book. What if it wasn't about the code book after all? Could it have been a single message meant for a different reality? Could that message have gotten caught during a time shift? They had never received a message telling them to buy the book. But maybe they had gotten a message urging them to finish reading the Arms Race in Time. How would he ever tell?

Andrew called his wife. She didn't answer so he left a message. "I miss you. It's safe to come home. I'll be here waiting for you. I'll be waiting for both of you."

The End

Reality chases Fiction

In 2011, I mused that entangled quantum particles looked a lot like a wormhole but only for information. If one somehow used a particle accelerator to propel half of the entangled pair at near light speed for an extended period of time, the two ends would become unstuck in time. The Standard Quantum Physics model allows for this.

In 2012, I wrote the first of three short stories in this collection, speculating how time mail could be used and how it might change society. One week after I published "Wasn't Tomorrow Wonderful", I read that two scientists at the Hebrew University of Jerusalem had succeeded at entangling quantum particles across time. Granted, the time difference was brief and the communication only went forward in time. Reading up on the team, there was nothing about how to construct an experiment to test if it is possible to send information backwards in time. Who knows. In a few decades maybe time mail will be more than just a story. And maybe someday I'll be a not-quite-forgotten author like the one in "The Arms Race in Time".

Science Now, 23 May 2013, "Physicists Create Quantum Link Between Photons That Don't Exist at the Same Time"

About the Author:

    John Stilwell was born and raised in the Midwest. In the 1980s, he was regularly published in popular computer magazines. He was a contributing author to three Commodore Computer books. He earned two degrees in Electrical Engineering. Today, he is an Engineer by day and an author and artist by night.

    He has traveled extensively overseas with his hobbies being various and regularly changing. They have ranged from studying massage to bungee jumping. In the 1990s, he learned to draw and produced a respectable quantity, selling an occasional piece.

    In the late 2000s, his daughter talked him into doing science projects together and documenting them as youtube.com videos. Some include a leaf blower powered one-man hovercraft, a solar powered hot air balloon cam and various magnetic levitation curiosities.

    By 2010, he was back into serious writing, focusing on books and articles.

Made in the USA
Middletown, DE
27 June 2018